Embarrassing Siblings,

Playground Taunts

and other Growing Pains.

By

Mayapee Chowdhury

First published in Great Britain in 2015

© Mayapee Chowdhury 2015
ISBN: 978-1-910115-42-8

Prepared for Publication by LionheART Publishing
House
Cover by Dave Johnson
Author Image by Tony Lyons

'For my family especially my siblings, Samyami and Rishii who were my childhood travel companions and inspired this book. Thank you also to the Phoenix Writers Group, Leicester for helping me to find my writing voice.'

Contents

Lassie from Barnsley

The only brown face,
People would stop and stare.
Walk the streets in a sari,
Feel like an alien.

Paki, brownie, blackie.
Heard it all.
Skin colour,
Automatic disqualification.

First day at school,
Lead in the school play
Bad idea!
With my broad northern accent.

Top that off with
Geeky glasses,
An unusual name,
Asking for trouble.

Still we blended in more
On Belgrave Road.
Masais in slippers and saris.

Still an identity crisis,
The turbulent adolescent years
I always remained
The Lassie from Barnsley.

The Near Miss Stop

'Excuse me. Binita, isn't it? Do you mind if I sit here?' asks Bolton Ashfield.

The most elusive bit of talent in school; this is the first time he's spoken to me. I'm amazed he knows my name. Of course I don't object to him sitting next to me but I know this is the closest I will ever get to him. He takes out a copy of *To Kill a Mocking Bird*, our set text for this term, which I'm enjoying. I attempt to start a conversation about the bus stops. My moment is lost as my tormentors, Hannah Ranson and Sonia Collins, get on the bus.

They walk by and raise their eyebrows at Bolton and blow him a kiss. Hannah Ranson spits her chewing gum at me: it lands on my jeans and they promptly press it in before it has chance to bounce off. Bolton looks in their direction and then helps me to get rid of the gum. It gets stuck to his hands in the process.

'You live the next street down from me, don't you?' he asks.

I shrug my shoulders and answer, 'Yeah, and . . .'

'Well, look, why don't you pop into mine? My mum knows a great technique to get chewing gum out of clothes. If you are not too rushed maybe we could chill out and watch *To Kill a Mocking Bird* on video?'

I rub my eyes to make sure this isn't a dream, that my worst enemies have actually helped me out.

My palms start sweating as we get near our stop. As I try to get off my seat I feel a pinching on my scalp, then hear a snorting snigger and turn round. My hair ribbon has been tied to the seat rail. When we reach our stop, Bolton gets up, grinning and shaking his head. He chats to the bus driver. That's my chance missed as I'm now stuck here with those two and never a hope of him ever speaking to me again. He must think I'm such a loser and how clever they are for playing that prank on me.

The bus comes to a halt but the driver switches off the engine, gets up and says, 'Right, you two, off my bus now! I'll be having words with your head teacher about this and will ask that you're banned from using the school bus service.'

As they are kicked off, Bolton and the bus driver help get the ribbon out of my hair, with Hannah and Sonia looking back in rage, and me smiling at them. Bolton and I walk off and head to his house, with those two still stomping from the extra walking they now have to do.

The Early Lesson

How typical of Mum to drop us off at the swimming baths early and get Miss Wright to keep an eye on us, so we can't skive the lesson. No chance of that with my hawk-eyed sister, Pinky, watching me.

Miss Wright introduces a new boy to the group: her son, Henson. Now I feel myself waking up a bit. I panic as I haven't shaved my legs. As Mum has dropped us off so early I just have time to make it to the chemist to grab some wax strips; they only need a slight patch up. What shall I do about Pinky though? If it was just me on my own I'd go and come back quickly, but the tittle-tattler will ask too many questions. Ok, it's worth a shot.

'Pinky, you stay here, I need to nip to the chemist.'

The expected response I get is, 'Why? You know Miss Wright won't let you. You're secretly buying make-up aren't you? You fancy that boy. Oooh, Bunty's in love, Bunty's in love.'

'Shut up, you rug rat!' I say to her, gritting my teeth.

'Girls, what's going on here?' calls out Miss Wright.

I try to get in first, then the brat replies, 'Bunty needs the chemist.' She then whispers to Miss Wright, 'Think it's, you know, that thing young ladies have, which I'm not supposed to know about.'

'No problem, I've got some out the back,' says Miss Wright.

I finally get a say. 'I'm actually allergic to those.'

Miss Wright looks at her watch. 'Well okay, I guess you're early, but you both go together and come straight back.'

So at least we have been allowed to pop out but I now have the task of buying the wax strips without the snitching rat seeing me. I have a plan, but let's get there first.

I walk into the chemist and head straight for the hair removers. Just when I think she isn't looking, the rug rat sneaks up behind me and says, 'Um, I thought you were getting stuff for your monthlies.'

'Do you have to call it "monthlies", and say it so loud? No harm in picking up some other bits too, as we're here so early.'

'Have you seen the queue? And look at the time.'

She's right but there's no way I'm letting Henson see my hairy legs. I go to the shortest queue. The number of people isn't the problem; it's how some people query the price of every item. We finally get out of there and make a run for the swimming pool. Now I have to remove the hair from my legs.

When I get to the changing rooms I waste no time and just apply the strips to the parts that need it. I'm sure I've missed some bits and I hurt myself and get clumps of wax on my legs from not smoothing the strips out properly before application.

'Come on, we'll be late! The class is going to start soon.'

As she tries to open the curtain I shout, 'No, don't come in!'

'Oh, I get it. Are you changing your tampon?'

'Yes I am, go and cover for me and I won't be long.'

When I get to the pool I have my sister to thank for not getting told off. I see Henson with his arm round another girl. I ask Miss Wright, 'Who's that girl?'

'Oh that's Henson's girlfriend, they've been together since primary school.'

My sister comes up to me and says, 'Plenty more fish in the pool. You'll be fighting them off with those smooth legs.'

I put my arm around my sister and give her a hug. 'Thanks for everything today, sis.'

In true brat fashion she replies, 'Well you better let me borrow that pink top and convince Mum to let me go to the cinema tonight.'

I splash water on her and say, 'You little brat.'

I step into the swimming pool and try to hide my pain; it was a bad idea to wax before getting into the water. My sister tells me what I've already worked out. 'Mum would tell you, let that be an early lesson to you not to put yourself through pain for a boy.'

Stripping Dreams

Shaping young minds,
And future citizens.
Laying down roots,
Lessons for life.

Watched in adoration,
To aspire to
The key to the future:
Hero worship.

To then find out
They are bigoted.
With preconceived judgments,
Only educated by certificates.

We live in the 21st century.
That doesn't matter.
Under a microscope,
Scrutiny for every move.

Hug a child too much,
You are possessive.
Not enough,
You are neglectful.

A child out of the ordinary
Does not fit the mould.
What a sin:
Daring to be different.

Ambition turned to mockery,
Made into satire.
Crushing a soul,
Burning a dream.

From a broken home.
That's still a stigma.
Put a hair out of place,
Let's call the social.

Targeting the wrong people.
By the book,
Politically incorrect paranoia.

Playground Battlefield

Leaving the warmth of my bed,
The cold day I would dread.
On awakening,
My heart thumping.

On entry,
A prayer.
Please don't pierce or wound,
With sharp words or objects.

No ally,
Joining the plot,
Standing alone
In the battlefield.

The last bell,
Air at last.
Quick getaway
To clean my wounds.

My head hits the pillow,
Relief. I survived.
Repetition of
Reliving it all the next day.

The Awakening

Awoke on a normal day
Ready for school.
Went to the bathroom.
I screamed.

Sight of blood,
I called my mother.
I am dying,
I am dying.

Shock for both.
It was announced:
You are a lady.
But I am only ten.

Five days a lifetime.
Boys and girls together,
Unable to hide.
They looked different.

They looked like children,
I became a woman.
Hairs on my body,
My ever-growing breasts.

Undress in hiding,
Using teachers' toilets.
Dreaded swimming.
Did a lot of skiving.

I went to bed a child,
Awakening a woman.
A sense of confusion
Who am I now?

Revelation

I manage to get beyond the school gates without a taunt or someone tripping me up. At one point I was actually considering a bulletproof vest to get me through the day. Today I'm commanding respect without even trying. People smiling, holding doors for me, saying hello: the actual eye contact is remarkable. It is, however, mainly from the male population of the school. I see the girls rolling up their skirts more and applying extra make-up as they look at me with venom.

I enter the form room with people helping me sit on my chair rather than pulling it from under me as usual. By force of habit now, I look behind me before placing my bum on the seat. Why the sudden change in status? Before Mrs Robin, our form tutor, enters the room the community's geek and golden boy, Arjun, approaches me with a rolled up magazine.

He whispers in my ear, 'Tut, Seema, this is the reason for your change in the popularity ranks. Make the most of it because in the eyes of our Asian community this is a scandal, and I will be right there when your parents find out.'

Throughout the day the respect continues as I'm the first to be picked for all teams and everyone wants to work with me during group assignments. The looks from Arjun continue: just my luck our families get on so well.

The last bell goes, for the end of school. I'm about to turn into a pumpkin. Arjun races ahead to my mum's car, laying on the charm. Worse still, his mother is also there, revelling in giving my mum the good news about my other life. Mum looks very happy; maybe it is just a front and she'll grill me at home in front of Dad.

She starts, 'Right, we need to get home quickly, we have a busy evening.' So Mum wants to get home early to discuss it with Dad. Here it comes. 'I was just talking to that lovely Arjun and his mother. They have invited us round for dinner.'

This sounds like typical Arjun; he wants to humiliate me in front of the whole family. The words 'I will be right there when your parents find out' echo in my ear. I know what, I'll just say I'm ill and try to get out of it.

'Seema, Seema,' Mum calls. I go downstairs, holding my stomach. Mum shakes her head, 'Look, we can't pull out now. If you really feel worse we'll just come home early.'

As we get to their house Arjun stands in the driveway with a grin on his face and his arms folded.

'Apologies, we're a bit late. Seema isn't feeling too well.'

As Arjun gives me a hug he whispers, 'Is that some faddy diet in your line of work that's made you ill?'

Even when snacks are served Arjun makes his little digs. 'Just water for you, I take it?'

Mum replies for me. 'That's right, Seema, if you're not well don't overdo the Bombay mix.'

Arjun adds, 'Yes, and Bombay mix is full of calories. Maybe cabbage soup for you.'

Mum squeezes Arjun's face. 'Such a considerate boy, and so knowledgeable. Then again you are going to be a doctor so you would know how to take care of Seema.'

'What are you going to be if, sorry when, you grow up, Seema?' asks Arjun.

Arjun's mother interrogates me further, 'Yes *beta,* you need to think about the future from now.'

Arjun takes his opportunity. 'Hmm, so many careers are short-lived these days. The ones where you have to rely on your looks, I mean.'

Can this evening get any worse? I think I need to start exaggerating my phantom illness more.

Finally we get to the end of dinner. Arjun has not said another word. We make our way to the living room and the adults start showcasing Arjun's medals.

He pulls my arm and takes me to one side, 'They won't notice we're gone, why don't we get popcorn and just chill for a bit?' For some reason Arjun seems eager to get away now. We sit in front of the TV and he hands the remote to me. I take the opportunity to catch up on *Roseanne*, and then try to change the channel.

'No, keep it on,' he tells me, with a change of tone in his voice. We sit through *Roseanne* and both laugh at the same bits. He then shows me a collection of other episodes on video. 'I doubt they'll come and get you any time soon so we might as well watch a few.'

Although I've been trying to escape from something this evening I get the feeling Arjun has too. I start to feel cold and he puts a blanket on me, attentive to my every need. Do I want another drink, am I not getting bored? I'm sure he has never been alone with a girl in his whole life.

'Seema, Seema!' my mother screams.

Before I leave Arjun takes my arm and says, 'Come over any time to watch *Roseanne* or just to get away from it all.'

As I leave I hug Arjun and whisper, 'Don't worry, your secret's safe, I won't tell anyone you watch *Roseanne*.' He laughs. As I get into the car, I look up and find Arjun by his bedroom window. He waves at me. This evening has been a quite a revelation, but not the one I expected.

Behind the Scenes

The scenic route of the Scottish Highlands distracts me from the awkward silence of the journey from Nottingham to Glasgow. A family weekend away that none of us are up for. We all have something to hide and need to invent a defence. With me it will be impossible to hide it. To stop the awkward silence we put on a CD. Why does the journey go by so quickly when you don't want to reach the destination? Mum insists on driving straight through rather than taking a break, which makes it worse.

When we get there the Porsches and Lexus vehicles are all neatly lined up. Cousin Laila comes out to greet us, decked out in all her diamante; you would think she'd bought the whole of Tiffany's. She starts on me, 'Dina, all skin and bones, you got worms? And where have you been all these months? Poor thing, you don't have a high metabolism like my Sunita.'

She moves on to my brother, Rikki. No hug for him; straight to the interrogation. 'Did you get into medicine?'

My dad doesn't even let him speak, but interjects, 'He's doing . . . doing law. It's a good profession, he could be a judge.'

'Ahh, never mind, Sunita's doing law too.'

So is Rikki is off the hook?

'At Camriss.'

Ah, never mind, Rikki. We assume she means Cambridge. Typical Laila; knows all the big designer brands, top university names but can't pronounce any of them.

It is like a maze to get through the door. 'Oh yes, we only got back from holiday last night. Dilip, he's such a romantic, always whisking me away for the weekend. We got back from Paris last night; look at the diamond he got me.'

We're shown to our rooms and wonder how we'll cope with a long weekend of all this. I decide to explore the stately maze. While I'm in the hallway I bump into Laila's husband, Dilip. I've always got on with him and actually feel sorry for him. He greets me with a hug and takes an interest in me by saying, 'You know you can always talk to me. It must have been tough in that clinic.'

He is summoned. I find myself in another bathroom. When I try to open the door to get out I realize it leads me to Laila and Dilip's room. How am I supposed to get out of here without them spotting me? From the gap through the door I see Laila trying to kiss Dilip, and him backing away.

Laila gets annoyed and asks, 'Have you started on that medication yet, or are you trying to avoid taking it in case it makes you want me?'

'Give us a chance, Laila.'

She storms off. Dilip checks to see she has gone and makes a phone call. In a low voice I hear him say, 'I'll try and get out tonight. Laila will hardly notice, she's too busy showing off in front of her family. Ok, same time same place, I need to see you, and I need to get away!'

Status

Rocked up in a Volvo,
Made to feel low
Before the school gate,
Even from my so-called mate.

All about status.
They caught the bus,
I could not comprehend,
My family was affluent.

Not from a council estate,
Taunted at same rate.
Why was I harassed,
And even embarrassed?

Excluded, pushed afar,
Just for a car.
Not even rust,
But status was a must.

Finding myself:
Being fat, being thin,
Look deep within.
What people want to see:
Is that really me?

No letters after your name,
What a shame.
All about rank and position,
Causing division.

Your skin is fair,
With luscious hair.
Have all the wealth,
Pointless without health.

I choose to be free
And live for me.
A lot to offer,
So with trivia why bother?

Be true to yourself,
That is your wealth.
You will get through,
Living a life that is true.

Love Lesson

Kids when we met,
My heart was set.
Seen with the ugliest in the school,
You felt a fool.

Out on a bike ride,
We would run and hide.
We would sneak,
A quick peck on the cheek.

You set me on fire,
Opened up my desire.
You would quench my thirst,
But you were my first.

I would get snappy,
My parents were not happy.
I would scream and shout
But they figured you out.

I could not see,
You used me.
Off with my best friend.
I could no longer pretend.

A journey of self-hate,
Purging to lose weight.
With self-destruction,
A lifetime of disruption.

Self esteem diminished,
I was finished.
Loathing what I saw,
Each and every flaw.

My Secret Gift

A prize for being ugly,
And famous for
My slow walk.

Never picked for a team
Or leading role.
Not pretty or clever,
And wrong skin colour.

That's what they thought.
Behind that,
I stood out
With purpose.

Leading by example,
Adored by all.
Inspiring youth
With my special gift.

Gift no longer hiding
Mocked by all:
The ugly Paki
Got the leading role.

In front of them
I stammered.
My throat went dry.
They were Right.

The whispers,
The sniggers.
She can't sing,
Bring back the pretty white girl.

The big day arrived,
Lights on me,
In front of them all
What if I fail?

Taking a deep breath
Sang my heart out,
Brought tears to eyes,
Leaving a high note.

Results Day

My friend got all 'A' stars,
Another is doing medicine,
The other is going to Oxford,
My life is over!

I must hide in shame,
How will I show my face again?
Law instead of medicine,
What a sin!

First major event,
Since the big day.
How many stars did you get?
I'm travelling to the moon.

Before you enter,
Show your CV,
And flashy car,
From your six figure salary.

Now an observer to all this,
I sit and ponder.
So much to learn about life,
This is not a problem!

Non-Uniform Day

Non-uniform day,
A lot to say:
The line of fire
Because of my attire.

Mocked by the school,
Made to look a fool.
My alleged friends,
They deserted me.

I looked at my watch,
The day dragged.
Treated like a parasite,
Sat in isolation.
Crying my eyes out,
What was the fuss about?
Having no voice,
And no choice.

Now they pass me in the street
And want to meet and greet.
Suddenly I'm good enough,
Outshining them all.

Not sponging from the state,
No excessive weight.
A sense of class,
Not a chav.

Getting pregnant as a child,
Contraction of a disease,
Robbed of my youth,
But I hold my head high.

Looking back,
I've come a long way,
And feel empowered:
A bully is a coward.

The Shopping Trip (up)

How typical! I never get to enjoy anything on my own. I'm about to become a young lady and I have to share it with my bratty brother. Dad was supposed to take him to a football match but we're getting used to him being a let-down. At the moment the shopping trip is going better than expected. Rikki and I aren't squabbling too much. He's been fuelled with a full tank of food, which helps.

We go into my shop first; Rikki is still quite calm about it. In the distance I see my new puberty rival, Kimmy. She looks busy and hasn't spotted me yet. I know what I need so if I just go to the changing rooms first then come out and grab stuff, I can be out of here before she spots me. Kimmy is a show-off who wants to flaunt her new body and what she can do with it. I'm trying desperately to buy a bra in hiding. She'll go mad if she sees me buying one; she can never know, otherwise my life will be over. I'd probably get blackmailed into not wearing it at school. She'd feel threatened with being stripped of her 'Big Tits' title, quite a status for someone like her.

After coming out of the changing rooms I walk around the shop almost feeling like a thief as it takes me ages to find what I need. I know you're supposed to get measured for these bras but I don't have the time. I'll bunch up a whole load of bras without even looking at the labels, and hope I'll find the right size.

Rikki keeps hovering with a grin on his face. What if the brat has figured out what I'm buying?

As I get closer to the lingerie section he sneaks up behind me and yells, 'There you go, Simi, this is the bra you were looking for.'

Kimmy looks straight over and it's hard to say who has the bigger shock. She comes over to me and says, 'Four Eyes! This doesn't mean you'll be in with us, and Andre is still my boyfriend.' She tries to hide something behind her back, then Rikki sneaks behind her, grabs it and shows it to me.

'Um, that's not even a real bra, it's got things stuffed inside it to make you look like you have boobies. You don't have real boobies!'

A couple of Kimmy's friends laugh and walk off after taking a good look at the bra. Kimmy then tries to lean up against her boyfriend, Andre. From the corner of his eye he glances at me and pulls away from Kimmy. Her friends nudge each other and walk away, laughing.

Andre lets go of Kimmy and disappears. Kimmy tries even harder to get up close to me, then Rikki calls out, 'Mum, Mum get her now. Some mad stuffed-bra girl is being horrible to Simi.'

Mum walks up to Kimmy. 'Oh yes, Kimmy, I know you. How are your lovely parents?' she says, with gritted teeth. 'I'll be seeing them next week at a school governors' meeting. I'll tell them we saw you in town with your friend.'

Kimmy storms off, and after she leaves Andre sneaks behind me and drops a note which has a phone number on it, and whispers, 'Come to the pictures tonight.'

Double Blind

The déjà vu of childhood. The classic 'geeky friend and gorgeous friend' scenario. I was the bookish, studious one, never interested in boys. Sharmaine was never without a man. Mind you, her striking good looks and celebrity status as a model helped. Sharmaine wanted me to settle down and meet someone, too. She was always fixing me up on blind dates, which ended in disaster. I was hoping it was now an abandoned mission. Sharmaine's heart was in the right place with good intentions. We've always remained best friends but she forgets it is possible to function without a man. People wonder why I've stuck to her all these years, considering the way she treated me.

No such luck regarding the Cupid fixation. Sharmaine had invited someone on a night out while she got frisky with her latest beau. He was a model like Sharmaine and they were parading magazine pictures where they posed together. Anyway I was more interested in the other tagalong she had brought. I looked closer and he seemed familiar but why couldn't I place him? He wouldn't have looked out of place in the magazines that Romeo and Juliet were parading. I hoped it was my blind date.

He nudged me with his elbow and nearly spilt a drink on me. 'I'm so sorry, I'll buy you another drink or top-up or even both. I'm so sorry.'

'Hang on, you're Benjamin Whimpiscle. My God, where have the glasses gone? Wow, you really scrub up well!'

'Tweesah, I could say the same about you, except for the fact that you are still hanging around with her. Very loyal.' We both looked over at Sharmaine and Lover Boy and rolled our eyes in unison. 'See, she's still not changed, trying to outdo you and show everyone she's the pretty one.'

I gave him a look.

'I'm so sorry, I'm not saying she's prettier, she's not. Under the slap and designer clothes there's no personality. I'm sorry, I'm bad at this.' That's one thing that hadn't changed about Ben. He was still clueless about how to talk to women. 'I don't want to watch the Sharmaine show all night, why don't we take a walk and catch up properly?' he suggested.

We caught up on the good old days but Ben didn't have a good word to say about Sharmaine and brought back some memories that I'd tried to block out such as when I got elected head girl and she still tried to outdo me by wiping dandruff from my shoulder in front of everyone and mocking my dress sense.

I laughed. 'I'm amazed you noticed all this, though, your head was always in a book.'

'I did notice you, though. Like me, you were bookish but you wanted to fit in. I liked you as you were, are, sorry.'

To stop him from making any more faux pas I leaned forward and kissed him on the lips, then moved away, thinking he would find it too forward. On the contrary, he carried on so I brought him inside. He couldn't hide his nerves. I wondered if it was his first time. I was certainly nervous he would notice it was mine! It is still slightly unheard of not to have your first time until you're almost twenty. Mind you, some Asians haven't moved into the twentieth century yet, and think sex is just for during marriage, with the lights turned out, in the missionary position for the purpose of making a baby. I thought maybe Ben was one of those more comfortable if the lights were turned out, so I put him at ease and told him, 'It's okay, let's just chill out and talk, I'll make us some coffee.'

When I went into the kitchen to make coffee, Sharmaine's boyfriend was there, and tried to kiss me. I poured the water on him and slapped him across the face. 'You're my best friend's boyfriend!' I screamed.

He laughed. 'Oh okay, so she's told you I'm her boyfriend?' He eventually got the message and backed off, slipping a card into my hand. 'Well, if you change your mind.' He smiled.

The business card showed that he was a model and escort. Shock, horror! I had to read it twice to check. When Sharmaine came into the kitchen I didn't say anything but poured her a drink and proposed a toast.

'What are we drinking to?' she asked.

'To double blind dates.' She knew what I meant as the business card was still lying on the table, though she thought I didn't notice her looking at it from the corner of her eye. How the tables had turned since childhood. The gorgeous model fighting the men off. Tonight not only did I pull, but got hit on too. Maybe I should think about fixing Sharmaine up on a blind date.

Safe Sex

Be grateful for what you have,
Don't end up a chav.
Youth is a gift,
Don't end up in a rift.

Life is possible,
But be responsible.
For a bit of fun,
End up all done.

Living self-deceit,
Trying to make ends meet.
Sponging from the system,
With no sense of rhythm.

Scrounging, is that your aim?
Well, what a shame.
Taxes we have paid,
So you can get laid.

With goodness in us,
What is the rush?
Why follow the crowd,
Be individual and proud.
A night of passion is great

At a cost to the state,
Have a bit of mettle,
For less do not settle.

You will get to forty
Then get shirty.
Life has passed you by
Ask yourself why?

Beating your friends in the race,
Of yourself no trace.
Stuck to someone like glue.
Who are you?

Reviews

If you enjoyed *Embarrassing Siblings, Playground Taunts and other Growing Pains*, please consider leaving a rating and review on Amazon. Reviews and feedback are important to an author, as well as other potential readers, and would be very much appreciated. Thank you.

About the Author

Mayapee Chowdhury is a versatile author of the critically acclaimed self help book *The Divorce Toolbox*, the children's rhyming picture book *Bye Bye Nursery* and *Flash Sex* under the pen name M S Devi. Mayapee also contributed one of her stories to an anthology put together by The Phoenix Writers Group Leicester. Mayapee grew up in South Yorkshire, Barnsley then later moved to Leicester where many of the poems and stories are set drawing from personal childhood experiences. Also a Spoken Word Artist Mayapee has performed at various festivals including Indian Summer and The Human Rights in Art and Film festival where she has mesmerized audiences with her thought provoking poetry, many of which are included in this collection.

To find out more about Mayapee and her work please visit her blog at
http://mummymanicmondays.blogspot.co.uk.

Mayapee is also very active on social media and you can follow her on Twitter: @Mayanishka or join her on Facebook:
https://www.facebook.com/mayapee.chowdhury

Other Books by Mayapee Chowdhury

The Divorce Toolbox

Bye Bye Nursery

Phoenix Square – An Anthology of Short Fiction
by Phoenix Writers Leicester

Under the pen name M.S. Devi

Flash Sex